Samuel French Acting Edition

Melancholy Play
A Contemporary Farce

by Sarah Ruhl

FOR PRODUCTION INQUIRIES

UNITED STATES AND CANADA
info@concordtheatricals.com
1-866-979-0447

UNITED KINGDOM AND EUROPE
licensing@concordtheatricals.co.uk
020-7054-7200

Each title is subject to availability from Concord Theatricals Corp., depending upon country of performance. Please be aware that *MELANCHOLY PLAY* may not be licensed by Concord Theatricals Corp. in your territory. Professional and amateur producers should contact the nearest Concord Theatricals Corp. office or licensing partner to verify availability.

MELANCHOLY PLAY was first produced by the Piven Theatre (Joyce Piven, Artistic Director) in Evanston, Illinois, on June 28, 2002. The production was directed by Jessica Thebus, with sets by John Dalton, lights by Lynne Koscielniak, costumes by Mary Trumbour, and sound by Micky York. The original music was composed by Gregory Hirte with additional songs by Jeffrey Weeter. Elizabeth Grantner was the stage manager and the cast was as follows:

TILLY . . . . Polly Noonan

FRANCES . . . . Amy Warren

LORENZO . . . . Scott Morton

FRANK . . . . Geoff Rice

JOAN . . . . Gita Tanner

CHARACTERS

FRANK – a tailor

TILLY – a bank teller

FRANCES – a hairdresser

JOAN – a British nurse

LORENZO THE UNFEELING – a psychiatrist

JULIAN – a musician

TIME

The present moment

PLACE

Illinois

NOTES

- Melancholy in this play is Bold, Outward, Sassy, Sexy, and Unashamed. It is not introverted. It uses, instead, the language of Jacobean direct address.

- Actors are encouraged to look out of the window often, climb in and out of windows, throw open balconies, throw themselves on couches.

- The pace is often faster than real time. Transitions should hurtle.

- Don't be afraid of sincere melodrama.

- The almond state is one of inert depression, of being encased and still, unlike the active state of melancholy, which yearns and moves. If one is inside an almond, one is not dead, though one might feel deadened. When one is reached by others inside an almond state, there is sincere joy all around.

THE SET

Many windows, a chaise, and several doors from which to enter and exit rapidly. A mirror. A potted palm. A chair. A few chandeliers. Or lamps. Perhaps a real balcony, opening into the night air.

COSTUMES

I imagine that Joan wears an old-fashioned nurse's uniform. Even though we are in Illinois, there is a sense of the iconic and cinematic.

THE MUSIC

The music exists in a parallel world, scoring Melancholy inside the head – an organ at a silent movie. It would be nice if the actor who plays Julian were from a country other than the United States. And he or she should be a very good cello player. And handsome, and brooding.

If possible, Julian is a man. If not, we are also very fond of women cello players.

FOREWORD

I've always been interested in the ancient category of emotional and aesthetic experience—melancholy—that has been a wellspring for artists from lyric poetry in Japan before the common era to Shakespeare to Robert Burton to the paintings of the 19th century to Rilke to Satie to Chopin to black and white movies. Melancholy can be active, yearning, hopeful, nostalgic, sexy even, and offers the possibility of communing with others. Melancholy makes us contemplate the inevitable passage of time—the transience of things—and in that sense, it's not neurotic, but rather part of the human condition.

Depression, by contrast, is hermetic, sealed off, inert, hopeless, an emotion hard to communicate to others; an emotion it would be nice to get rid of. I felt that in our cultural zeal to eradicate depression in the current pharmaceutical era (as well we should) that possibly other shades of emotion were getting eased out of the language and the culture at the same time—and perhaps it wasn't worth throwing the baby out with the bathwater.

So I wrote *Melancholy Play*, in which a woman is so drenched in a sensual melancholy that everyone falls in love with her. Then one day she gets happy, wreaking havoc on her paramours. One woman—Frances—falls into such a depression over her lost love that she turns into an almond. Twelve years later, I met a wonderful composer named Todd Almond. Freud says there are no coincidences.

I always felt there might be more music in the play, and Todd said he heard a string quartet, piano, and an almost sung through score. I trusted Todd implicitly—he has gorgeous green eyes that look as though they are always dreaming of some far off sea—he is from the Midwest, as am I—and his music is beautiful. He wrote the score, effortlessly flinging the music into song, and here is our offering to you.

The other question the play poses is how to reach people who are sealed off—past the point of melancholy, and in a windowless room of depression. The rather simple answer that the play offers is: you go to them. Thank you for traveling to the country of melancholy with us. We take the journey seriously, but we hope that you have some serious fun along the way.

– Sarah Ruhl, 2015

This play is dedicated to everyone who, at one point or another, has traveled to an almond state.

***

The *amygdala* (Greek for almond, because it happens to be almond shaped) lies anterior to the hippocampus in the brain. The amygdala attaches affective color and social meaning to sensory information; it also receives primary olfactory input which accounts for the major role that olfaction plays in emotion and behavior. The amygdala plays a key role in the startle reflex and can generate flight or fight responses. The amygdala also helps regulate appetite, mood, aggressive and sexual behavior, social behavior, and comprehension of social cues. Auras from partial seizures arising in the amygdala can cause olfactory sensations – for example: the smell of bitter almonds.

***

From Robert Burton's *Anatomy of Melancholy*, 1632:

"Amongst its many inconveniences, some comforts are annexed to Melancholy: First, it is not catching…"

PART 1

Frank offers up his defense

FRANK. (*to the audience*) I would like to propose to you – this
evening – a defense of melancholy.

Cello music from Julian.

Proposition 1 –
That melancholy is a necessary bodily humor –
that there is a certain amount of necessary mourning –
due to things that grow and pass –
rice, the moon, wheat, childhood, ment's hats, tides on
a marsh, fingernails –
Which leads me to:

Proposition 2:
That melancholy
is a disappearing emotion –
there is no place for it in the afternoon –
out the window – to observe the passage of time –
we are depressed –
but are we melancholy?
Are we capable of melancholy?
Which leads me to:

Proposition 3:
if disavowed –
the repressed melancholia may lead to other
disturbances of the mind –
may I here remind you of the god-mother who was not
invited to sleeping beauty's baptism –

she took revenge.
She took revenge!

Proposition 4:
That we must anatomize melancholy –
take stock of the causes:
stars a cause
love a cause
death a cause
morning a cause
afternoon a cause
evening a cause
the odd times in between morning afternoon and
evening:
a cause.

> *No more cello music.*

> *Frank looks out the window.*

> *He raises the blind.*

Tilly asks Frank why he is like an almond

Tilly walks up to Frank.

Frank's back is to Tilly.

She taps him on the back.

Frank turns around.

TILLY. Why are you like an almond?

They look at the audience.

They exit.

The Unfeeling Lorenzo

Lorenzo has an unidentifiable Italian accent.

LORENZO. My name is Lorenzo.
You would think,
with a name like Lorenzo,
that I would feel great passions.
Sadness, violent anger,
unbridled lust.
But my lust is bridled or not at all.
My anger too is bridled.
And my sadness – there is a cap on it, so it cannot get out.

Lorenzo, who plays the harp, in the dark, you might think.
Lorenzo, with kisses like Mediterranean apples, you might think.

But no.

It is I: Lorenzo, the unfeeling.
The Unfeeling Lorenzo.
I am an orphan. I was found on the door-step of a candy store.
I was raised on sweets, in an unspecified European country.
I felt myself to be European.
I spoke an unspecified European language.
I lived on a street with cobblestones.
I wore a tan scarf.
But I did not suffer like a European.
No. I was – happy.

One day my long-lost
mother appeared on the steps of the sweet-shop.
She was wearing a black skirt and black gloves
and a little black veil.

I smiled at her.

My God, he smiles like an American! she said.
Like he's smiling for a picture!
How white his teeth are!
And how straight!
(It was very disconcerting,
as you might imagine,
for my mother.)

How could I have given birth, she said,
to this child?
Suffering, she announced,
is a brand of citizenship!
Then she walked out the door.

So I moved to Illinois.
I feel – normal here.
People say: you have such understanding eyes,
Lorenzo.
I look into your eyes and I feel I can deposit my pain
right there – like a coin, into a hole.
I have an office.
It is here.
Come in.

    Tilly enters Lorenzo's office.

LORENZO. So.

TILLY. So.

LORENZO. You went off the medication.

TILLY. Yes. I'm sorry about that.

LORENZO. Uh-huh. You're sorry. Good. So.
How are we feeling today?

TILLY. I don't know how you are feeling. I am feeling –
melancholy.

LORENZO. And what does that feel like?

TILLY. I would like to die and be reborn as a mushroom.

I would like to stay warm and slightly damp.

I will release spores now and again when it suits my mood.

LORENZO. Tilly. I want for you to go on a new medication. It is a very good medication. It will make you feel – very nice.

TILLY. Lorenzo. Can I call you Lorenzo?

LORENZO. Lorenzo is my name. Yes, it is!

TILLY. Lorenzo.

Cheerful people are the worst sort of people. They make noise when they smile. Their teeth have little bells between the cracks. When they smile, their teeth ring.

LORENZO. I am going to fold my arms now Tilly. (*He does.*) It seems to me, Tilly, that you don't want to get better. It seems to me that you enjoy this "melancholy" of yours. In fact, you seem proud of it. A little vain, even. It is my professional opinion that you feed your melancholy little sweet-meats, that you comb it, groom it, keep it as a pet dog. Why have you come to see me?

TILLY. The bank made me come. They don't like their employees to be melancholic.

LORENZO. But you – you like to be a melancholic employee.

TILLY. Not really. I'd rather work for myself. Open a shop. Perfume. Or hats.

LORENZO. Let me tell you a story, Tilly. A patient of mine – he thought if he urinated, he would flood his entire village. So he could not urinate! And this was very painful to him. So I tell him a little white lie, I say to him, sir your whole village is on fire. And suddenly he feels free to urinate. He feels, through this ordinary physical activity, that he is saving his village again and again.

TILLY. Huh.

LORENZO. Are you afraid of putting out the fires?

TILLY. No.

LORENZO. Do you find me attractive, Tilly? Is that the problem?

TILLY. I don't think so.

LORENZO. We call it transference, Tilly.

TILLY. At the bank you can transfer money – from one account – to another. I don't do that.

LORENZO. It is normal to fall in love with me. It is "okay."

TILLY. I am not in love with you!

LORENZO. Okay. Okay!

TILLY. Lorenzo: why do you try to make people happy?

LORENZO. Because I, myself, am happy. Happiness is contagious. It's like a disease.

TILLY. Do you never long to be sad?

LORENZO. No.

TILLY. Do you never want to cry?

LORENZO. No!

A pause.

The sound of rain.

TILLY. It's raining out.

LORENZO. So it is.

TILLY. Let's put our hands in the rain.

They open the window and stick their hands out, feeling the rain.

Sad, stirring music, played by Julian, on the cello.

Look at the rain – how it sticks to the flowers. There's a word in Japanese for being sad in the spring-time – a whole word just for being sad about how pretty the flowers are and how soon they're going to die – I can't remember the word –

LORENZO. You are a very beautiful woman.

TILLY. Oh no.

LORENZO. Tilly – my mother abandoned me at a sweet-shop.

TILLY. Why are you telling me this?

LORENZO. Because – the heavens have cracked open – I suddenly want to tell you everything. I think I'm in love with you, Tilly. They say that's what happens when you fall in love. You want to tell people things. You especially want to tell them sad things. Hidden sad things from the past. Something like: I was abandoned at a sweetshop in an unspecified European country. Tilly.

TILLY. I'm so sorry.

LORENZO. Don't be sorry. I want to tell you all the sad things, and then – you will know me better than other people know me and that means we are reserved for one another. Because we made a reservation like at a restaurant like at a grand hotel and we made this reservation with a certain foreign currency made of secret sad information we told each other in private rooms – Oh, I feel a weight on my chest. What have you done to me, Tilly? Why?

TILLY. I'm sorry, Lorenzo. This happens sometimes – to me. I should have warned you.

Frank and Frances' Account of their Labor

Frances and Frank speak simultaneously when their text is written on corresponding lines; otherwise, they pause. They gesture in parallel fashion.

They address the audience.

FRANK.	FRANCES.
When I gave up accounting	When I gave up physics
	I found myself sitting in public places
I found myself sitting in public places	
	libraries, restaurants, movie theaters
I pretended	
	that I was accountable
to the other people in the room	
	and that furthermore
they were accountable	
	to me.
I lost my watch.	I lost my watch.
I didn't buy a new one.	I didn't buy a new one.
I enjoyed asking strangers:	
What time is it?	
	What time is it?
	And they always answered.
11 o'clock.	2 o'clock.

(They turn towards one another.)

Thank you, I said.	Thank you, I said.

(They turn away.)

This could be repeated   This could be repeated
over and over again.   over and over again.

(They turn towards one another.)

What time is it?   What time is it?
11 o'clock.

                                    Thank you.

You're welcome.

(They turn away.)

So reassuring.   So reassuring.
To experience   To experience
the social contract –   the social contract –
again and again.   again and again.

And so I became a tailor.   And so I opened a
                                    beauty salon.

Even when I was a child   Even when I was a child
I liked it   I liked it
when strangers touched   when strangers touched
me   me
with clinical purpose –   with clinical purpose –
people I was not related   people I was not related
to.   to.

Comforting –   Comforting –
the hem of my pants   my hair – wet –
soft against my leg   soft against my shoulders
a stranger who cared   a stranger who cared
or seemed to care   or seemed to care
about my physical   about my physical
well-being.   well-being.
Not creepy, understand –

                                    nothing untoward
                                    or perverse –
but gentle.   but gentle.

I could have been
a prostitute
and gotten the
same effect
or a doctor maybe –
but no
the touch should
feel – off-hand

I could have been
a prostitute
and gotten the
same effect
or a doctor maybe –
but no
the touch should
feel – off-hand –
someone grazes
your shoulder
while they're
doing something else –

(The speed of their speech slows down slightly.)

something peaceful
no big deal
time slows down
when you're
hemming pants…

something peaceful
no big deal
time slows down
when you're
cutting hair…

(Pause.)

Plus I like fabric
I've always liked fabric
how it looks
how it smells
how it hangs
how a good suit
can improve
an ugly duckling's
appearance
make them feel
competent
and unafraid.

Plus I like hair
I've always liked hair
how it looks
how it smells
how it hangs
how a good haircut
can improve
an ugly duckling's
appearance
make them feel
competent
and unafraid.

Tilly goes to the tailor

Tilly stands in front of the mirror.

She wears trousers underneath her gown.

Frank pins the hem of her pants leg.

TILLY. Why are you like an almond?

FRANK. Sorry?

TILLY. I wanted to ask you.

FRANK. You wanted to ask me –

TILLY. Why are you like an almond?

FRANK. Did you ask me this before?

TILLY. Yes. Three seconds ago.

FRANK. I mean another time? Further back? I'm having a sensation of *déjà vu.*

TILLY. I hate *déjà vu.* Do you want to sit down?

FRANK. No, that's okay. Can you tell me <u>why</u> I am like an almond?

TILLY. You are like an almond because
you are dry – like bark –
a hungry woman doesn't stuff her mouth with almonds
they don't fill a person up –
you eat one and your mouth goes dry –
like the moment before you want to kiss someone –

FRANK. Have we met somewhere – before I was hemming your trousers?

TILLY. I work at the bank.

FRANK. Oh!

TILLY. I give you your money. You ask for forty dollars. I give it to you in two tens and one twenty.

FRANK. That sounds familiar.

TILLY. I put the money in your hands. You are always distracted. When you leave, I watch you go. You always turn left.

FRANK. I do. I do turn left.

TILLY. I'm not mistaken then, It's you that we're discussing.

FRANK. Yes, I think it's me that we're discussing –

TILLY. Why do you always deposit your check in person? You can deposit the check into a machine. Outside. Do you know that?

FRANK. Yes – I'm aware of that.

TILLY. So then why –

FRANK. I don't know. It's just what I've always done.

TILLY. I never use the machine either.

FRANK. You don't?

TILLY. No. I don't.

(They look at each other.

Frank looks away.)

Are you afraid of me?

FRANK. No – I don't think so.

(Tilly moves and Frank jabs himself with a pin.)

Ouch!

Sorry.

TILLY. Do you think I want to crack you open with a mallet and look inside you?

FRANK. No.

TILLY. Because that's exactly what I'd like to do to you.

FRANK. Look – I'm a tailor – I –

TILLY. I mean not in a violent sense. Just in the sense that – I have a Persian friend. He once said to me – American men only have two emotions: happy and mad.

(Frank stops tailoring.)

FRANK. I'm not like that.

TILLY. I know.

You get sad – just by looking at the way light comes in through the window. In the afternoon maybe.

FRANK. I do.

TILLY. You do?

FRANK. I do. What's wrong?

TILLY. It's just that –

Everyone is always coming and going.
I wish they would stay in one place.
At the bank – after they get their money –
customers – leave.
I stay – I stay there all day!
I think – that they think –
that I disappear until the next transaction –
well I don't! I stay!
In the mind of God – everything happens –
perpetually – God thinks about us all the time,
he keeps us alive, just by thinking about us –
well that's like me!
I THINK ABOUT MY CUSTOMERS ALL THE TIME.

She is on the verge of tears.

FRANK. I'm so sorry.

TILLY. No, you're not!

FRANK. I am, really! You seem – a little – sad – are you – sad?

TILLY. Sometimes.

FRANK. I don't mind. I like that, actually.

A pause. They look at each other.

Stirring sad music, played by Julian, on the cello.

TILLY. There's a word in Portuguese – I can't remember the name – it means melancholy – but not exactly – it means you are full of longing for someone who is far away –

FRANK. I know that word.

TILLY. What is it.

FRANK. I can't remember.
Kiss me.

TILLY. You don't even know my name.

FRANK. What is your name?

TILLY. Tilly.

FRANK. Kiss me, Tilly.

TILLY. I don't know if that would be appropriate. You're hemming my trousers –

FRANK. You're right.
It would be highly inappropriate.

> *They look at each other.*
>
> *Tilly's trousers fall down.*
>
> *They kiss.*
>
> *A tableau.*

Tilly visits Lorenzo

Lorenzo interrupts the tableau.

LORENZO. So – you kissed this – Frank – while he was hemming your trousers.

TILLY. Yes.

LORENZO. I see. Did he kiss like an American? Were his lips hard? Did he move his tongue around like a tractor turning over the earth?

TILLY. Ah – no.

LORENZO. Did you hear music – inside your head – when you kissed him?

TILLY. No.

LORENZO. So it's nothing serious.

TILLY. Is the bank paying for this?

LORENZO. Tilly. I AM SUFFERING!
Look into my eyes.
Can you see the suffering?

TILLY. Yes.

Tilly helps Lorenzo onto the chaise.

LORENZO. Ever since I met you, there has been no morning and no evening.
There is only one long afternoon.
The afternoon is shaped like an almond.
Every day I think I will step into the almond like a boat and ride it into evening.
But I lie down in the almond boat
and it is always afternoon.
I look up and there is no piazza –
there are no old men to play cards with
who know my family name.

TILLY. I understand, Lorenzo.

LORENZO. You do?

TILLY. I'll play cards with you.

LORENZO. Is that American for: I will be your bride?

TILLY. No.

> *Lorenzo moans quietly.*

But I will play cards with you. And look out the window with you. Then I have to get my hair-cut.

LORENZO. You are cutting off your hair!

TILLY. Just a little bit.

LORENZO. No!

TILLY. Yes!

LORENZO. NO!

TILLY. YES!

LORENZO. Why?

TILLY. I need a trim.

LORENZO. But your hair – it is the sad song of a lark!

TILLY. Lorenzo. Be calm. It's just a trim. We will play cards. I am an old man. You are an old man. We live in Italy. We drink out of small cups. There is time for us to gaze out over the mountains and think about the past. You will think about your mother. I will think about my mother. But we will say nothing. We will play cards. Okay?

LORENZO. Will you save me the hair? From your hair-cut?

TILLY. Sure.

LORENZO. Can I touch your hair, before you go?

TILLY. Okay.

> *She lets him bury his face in her hair.*

LORENZO. Oh! If only my whole being were just one big nose, to smell you always with.

> *A tableau.*

Frances cuts Tilly's hair

Frances holds a mirror up to the back of Tilly's head.

FRANCES. You like it so far?

TILLY. Yes.

Frances cuts Tilly's hair some more.

TILLY. I love this beauty shop.

FRANCES. Thank you.

TILLY. Is it all yours?

FRANCES. Yes, I own it.

TILLY. I walk past it every night, on the way home. I look in the window. When it's all shut down, and the lights are off.

FRANCES. Really?

TILLY. Yes. At night – it's so beautiful – and empty, and sad. All the hair is swept off the floor – as in: a woman has gone home for the night.

There are plastic vestments draped on chairs
to catch the useless things that have fallen.

FRANCES. I'd never thought of it like that –

TILLY. There is a neon sign in the window – it is in earnest about beautification.

FRANCES. You think my sign is earnest?

TILLY. In a good way.

FRANCES. It sounds like you've – thought about it.

TILLY. I have.

FRANCES. Your hair is incredibly healthy.

TILLY. I don't use conditioner. And I don't blow dry it.

FRANCES. That's good. You should keep that up.

TILLY. Do women tell you lots of secrets when you cut their hair?

FRANCES. Stories you wouldn't believe.

TILLY. I thought so. Like what?

FRANCES. I can't tell.

TILLY. When I pass your beauty shop – at night – I imagine all the stories women have told during the day – holding court in green light. Stories with tiaras. And green wands. I'm sorry. Sometimes I get wound up. Then I tell people what I'm thinking.

FRANCES. So – what do you do?

TILLY. I work at a bank.

FRANCES. Really?

TILLY. Yes, why.

FRANCES. You don't seem like you work at a bank.

TILLY. What are you saying about banks?

FRANCES. Ah…

TILLY. Or – what are you saying about me?

FRANCES. I –

TILLY. You must have meant something by it.

FRANCES. Really, I didn't.

(A pause. Tilly looks hurt.)

Is anything wrong?

TILLY. No. I'm fine.

Frances finishes the haircut.

FRANCES. Well, I'm finished. Do you want to see?

TILLY. Oh no…

FRANCES. What's wrong?

TILLY. I hate for it to be over.

FRANCES. Well, I could comb it for five more minutes.

TILLY. That would be heaven.

FRANCES. Okay.

(Frances combs Tilly's hair.)

TILLY. Were you always a hairdresser?

FRANCES. No – a physicist.

TILLY. Really?

FRANCES. Yes.

TILLY. All those angles.

FRANCES. Yes.

TILLY. Then what?

FRANCES. I gave it up.

TILLY. Are you happier now?

FRANCES. Yes, I think so.

TILLY. That's good.

     (Frances combs Tilly's hair.)

Do you ever feel melancholy, in the afternoon, sweeping up the hair that's no longer on anyone's head?

     The stirring of music, played by Julian on his cello.

     The lights dim.

FRANCES. Sometimes.

TILLY. I feel like I can smell the ocean.

FRANCES. I feel like I can smell the ocean too!

TILLY. Right now?

FRANCES. Right now!

TILLY. Wow!

FRANCES. How about that?

TILLY. All the way from Illinois!

FRANCES. I can smell sea-weed.

TILLY. I can smell salt.

FRANCES. Mmm.

TILLY. Are you from the ocean?

FRANCES. I used to live by the ocean.

TILLY. Oh – so you're far from home.
     You're in – exile?

FRANCES. Well – I moved. From New Jersey.

TILLY. The wind is different by the ocean, isn't it?

FRANCES. I think so.

TILLY. Do you ever collect it – all that lost hair?

FRANCES. No. What would I use it for?

TILLY. Oh, nothing. So it wouldn't be left alone. So it would be with the other lost hair. Do you mind if I keep my hair?

FRANCES. No, that's fine.

TILLY. I love this time of afternoon.

FRANCES. Me too.

TILLY. Me too.

FRANCES. Me too.

TILLY. Me too.

FRANCES. Uh-oh.

TILLY. What?

FRANCES. I have a nurse at home. She wouldn't like me to say "Me too" three times in a row.

TILLY. She takes care of you?

FRANCES. Well – kind of. I live with her.

TILLY. Oh. There's a word in Russian – it means melancholy – but not exactly – it means to love someone but also to pity them.

FRANCES. You really do have beautiful hair.

> *Tilly and Frances look at each other.*

> *Tilly puts her hand on Frances' cheek.*

> *Tilly rips off her plastic hair vestment and hands it to Frances.*

> *A brief tableau.*

Lorenzo the Unfeeling from Behind a Window

LORENZO. (*as Tilly and Frances part.*)
Causes of Love Melancholy:
Temperature, Idleness, Diet.

Beauty from the Face,
Beauty from the Torso,
Beauty from the Eyes, and other parts.

Of all causes the remotest are stars.
Oh, Tilly. Why?

Frances explains to Joan about her affair with Tilly

FRANCES. You're asking me – what she's like?

JOAN. Yes.

FRANCES. It won't make you feel funny if I tell you?

JOAN. I feel funny already.

FRANCES. What do you want to know about her?

JOAN. The usual things.

FRANCES. You're not going to get upset.

JOAN. No.

FRANCES. She's – delicate. She could spend an entire afternoon filling a bowl with water, and putting yellow flowers into the bowl.

JOAN. So – she's a hard worker.

FRANCES. Well…she's – tired – but in this – seductive way.

JOAN. I don't understand.

FRANCES. She makes her unhappiness into this sexy thing. She throws herself onto couches.

JOAN. You wanted to take care of her.

FRANCES. Yes – I did.

JOAN. She seemed – spontaneous.

FRANCES. Yes.

JOAN. With a name like "Tilly" –

FRANCES. Yes.

JOAN. Oh. I see.

FRANCES. I didn't want to upset you.

JOAN. I'm not upset. I'd like to meet her.

FRANCES. I don't know if that's a very good idea.

JOAN. We'll have tea. It will be civilized. I'm not a jealous person, Frances. You know that.

Frank and Tilly

FRANK. *(to the audience)*   **TILLY.** *(to the audience)*
  I took Tilly home to   I took Frank home to
  my apartment.   his apartment.
  I said: He said:

FRANK. You are like – a painting –

TILLY. What painting?

FRANK. I don't know.
  The one where a woman
  looks sad and beautiful.

TILLY. Like this?

    (a demonstration)

FRANK. Yes.
  Only –
  your head goes over your shoulder,
  a little to the left.
  With your chin down.
  And your eyes looking up.
  Your eyes should look hopeful.
  while your chin looks sad.
  One thing goes up,
  one thing goes down.
  Yes.
  Oh,
  yes.
  I wish I could paint you.

TILLY. Why don't you?

FRANK. I can't paint.

    Frank and Tilly approach the audience.

FRANK.   **TILLY.**
  Then we made love.   Then we made love.
  Under the covers.   Under the covers.
  The whole thing!

TILLY. The room was dark,

FRANK. the sheets were damp,

   it was everything I'd hoped for.

TILLY. And afterwards,

FRANK.	TILLY.
I held her in my arms.	I held him in my arms.
It was like a movie.	It was like a movie.
An aerial shot.	An aerial shot.
Her head on my chest.	His head on my chest.
Then she gazed up at me –	Then he gazed up at me –
I said –	he said –

FRANK. Play the sea-sick music.

   I'm in love.

     A pause. Julian begins to play love-lorn music. He
     stops.

TILLY. Wait – don't say that.

FRANK. Why?

TILLY. I'm scared.

FRANK. She said.

   What are you scared of?

   I asked.

TILLY. Have you ever seen what sadness looks like on a
person, once they take off their grey shoes and grey
gloves? It looks different. Not like a movie. People wear
sweatpants when they are sad in private. Not pearls.
You won't like it.

FRANK. That's not possible. Tilly. I love you.

TILLY & FRANK. We breathed together in the dark for a
long time.

FRANK.
Then she began to cry.

TILLY.
Then I began to cry.

FRANK.
She was beautiful when she cried.

TILLY.
I'm beautiful when I cry.

I don't get in trouble with policemen when I cry.

FRANK.
Oh, Tilly.

TILLY. Oh, Frank.

FRANK. Oh, Tilly.

TILLY. Oh, Frank.

FRANK. Oh, God.

TILLY. God has no part in this.

FRANK. I'm sorry.
Oh, Tilly.

TILLY. Oh, Frank.

FRANK. Oh, Tilly.

TILLY. Wait – don't say my name again.

FRANK. What?

TILLY. Don't say it, I think.

FRANK. But I've been saying it.

TILLY. But now it's wrong.

FRANK. I don't understand.

TILLY. The first three times you said it right, the fifth time it felt – questionable – the sixth time wrong. That Tilly was not me.

FRANK. I said your name wrong?

TILLY. You *thought* my name wrong. You experienced a person who was not me. Then you spoke that person's name.

FRANK. I see.

TILLY. Try again.

FRANK. Tilly.

TILLY. No.

FRANK. Tilly.

TILLY. Closer.

FRANK. Tilly.

TILLY. Let's stop. Frank. Religious people don't address God directly in their prayers. They have a nickname for Him. So they don't get it wrong. That's why when you love someone you don't use their proper name. You call them something else. Like honey or spooky or shlumpy or little spoon. Do you understand me?

FRANK. Why are you so mean to me, Tilly?

TILLY. I don't know. Am I mean to you? I love you.

FRANK. You do?

TILLY. Yes.

Tell me something sad about your past. It will make us feel better. It will make us feel like we know each other.

FRANK. Okay, let me think.

A pause.

They turn towards the audience.

I told Tilly something
sad
about my past.
Not the saddest thing, but
fairly sad.

TILLY.

I felt that I understood
him.

We cried, at the same
time.
I offered her my
handkerchief.

We cried, at the same
time.

(He gives her a handkerchief)

You are the only man I
have ever

met who still carries a
handkerchief!
I love you!

(They embrace.)

Tilly thought for three
hours about:

the lost Art   the lost Art
of the Handkerchief   of the Handkerchief

until she fell asleep.

I watched her sleep.
A strange desire came over me
to save her tears, forever.
I wrung out the handkerchief
into a little vial.
And I watched her sleep, all night.

Joan and Frances and Tilly have Tea

They sip their tea. Joan looks Tilly over.

JOAN. Would you like some more *hot water?*

TILLY. No thank you.

FRANCES. Would anyone care for a little tea sandwich shaped like a triangle?

TILLY. I like triangles.

FRANCES. Good, then. Joan, pass the triangle shaped sandwiches.

JOAN. Certainly.

TILLY. MMM – this triangle shaped tea sandwich is good. What –

> *(a little pause)*

is on it?

FRANCES. Canned asparagus and mayonnaise. It's a real treat in New Zealand.

TILLY. I've never been to New Zealand.

JOAN. I've never been to New Zealand either. Out of the three of us, only Frances has been to New Zealand. That means we have something in common, Tilly.

TILLY. More than one thing, I would imagine, Joan.

FRANCES. It's lovely weather we're having.

TILLY. Unseasonably warm.

JOAN. You're just a young thing, aren't you?

TILLY. I'm fairly young – yes.

JOAN. I think that's wonderful, to be young.

TILLY. I'm sad most of the time.

JOAN. But it's wonderful to be young.

TILLY. Yes – you're right – it is wonderful.

JOAN. Don't get old.

TILLY. You're hardly old. My goodness.

JOAN. You have beautiful eyes. Doesn't she, Frances?

TILLY. You do too.

JOAN. Do you think so? Really?

TILLY. Yes.

JOAN. No.

TILLY. Oh, yes. Here – let me look.

Tilly approaches Joan's face and looks into her eyes.

You have orange rings around the pupils –

JOAN. Frances – I have orange rings in my eyes!

FRANCES. I heard.

JOAN. Don't you think that's marvelous?

FRANCES. Yes, Joan.

JOAN. Frances, close your eyes and tell me what color my eyes are.

FRANCES. I know what color your eyes are.

JOAN. She sounds testy, doesn't she?

TILLY. Are you upset, Frances?

JOAN. She gets this way.

FRANCES. I love to be talked about in the third person.

JOAN. She hates to be talked about in the third person.

TILLY. It's such a beautiful dining room you have.

JOAN.	FRANCES.
Thank you.	Thank you.

TILLY. The wallpaper is so gorgeous.

JOAN. Until I met Frances, I hated wallpaper.

TILLY. Really? Why?

JOAN. It reminded me of covered up things. Blood-stains.

TILLY. Of course –

JOAN. Girls who wear pearls. White and blue floral patterns.

TILLY. Yes – I can see that.

JOAN. But Frances grew up with wallpaper. She likes it. Don't you Frances?

FRANCES. You're so talkative today, Joan.
She's usually shy.

JOAN. That's true. I'm a very shy person.

TILLY. I think that's nice. To be shy.

JOAN. Thank you.

TILLY. I think it's interesting when a shy person says "I'm a shy person." Because it's not a very shy thing to say.

JOAN. That's true. I hadn't thought of that.

TILLY. Or when a person says: "I'm not a self-absorbed person." Isn't it funny when someone says that? Because they're – you know – talking about themselves?

> *(Joan and Frances laugh.)*

Or when someone says: "Do you think I'm insecure?" Do you get it – because if they have to ask –

> *(Joan and Frances laugh.)*

I always find that funny. When people say those things.

> *(Pause.)*

I'm dating a man named Frank now. He's a tailor.

FRANCES. Frank?

TILLY. Yes – Frank. Isn't that a beautiful name? Like Frankfurter. Sort of American. I love the smell of hot-dogs. At a baseball game.

> *(Pause. They look at her.)*

Do you ever have the feeling, when you wake up in the morning, that you're in love but you don't know with what?

JOAN.	FRANCES.
Yes!	Yes!

> *They look at each other, irritated.*

TILLY. It's this feeling that you want to love strangers, that you want to kiss the man at the post-office, or the woman at the dry-cleaners – you want to wrap your arms around life, life itself, but you can't, and this feeling wells up in you, and there is nowhere to put this great happiness – and you're floating – and then you fall down and become unbearably sad. And you have to go lie down on the couch.

JOAN.	FRANCES.
Are you still in therapy Tilly?	I know what you mean.

They look at each other, irritated.

FRANCES. Are you still in therapy?

TILLY. That's funny. Everyone is always asking me: Tilly, are you still in therapy? I say something like: I had a bad day. And they say: Tilly, are you still in therapy? I go to therapy and my therapist falls in love with me. I have to be careful.

JOAN. How so?

Tilly moves towards the audience. Her speech becomes a public speech. Stirring music from Julian.

TILLY. I'm not particularly smart.
I'm not particularly beautiful.
But I suffer so well, and so often.
A stranger sees me cry –
they see a river they haven't
swum in –
a river in a foreign country –
so they take off their trousers
and jump in the water.
They take pictures
with a water-proof camera
they dry themselves in the sun.
They're all dry
and I'm still wet.

Maybe my suffering is from another time.
A time when suffering was sexy.
When the afternoons, and the streets,
were full of rain.
Maybe my tears don't come from this century.
Maybe I inherited them from old well water.

The music stops.

Wait.

Am I acting weird?

JOAN & FRANCES. No, no.

TILLY. I'm sorry. Do you mind if I lie on your couch for a moment? I'm feeling sort of –

(She feels melancholy.)

JOAN & FRANCES. Please do.

Tilly lies down on their couch. They look at her.

They stroke her hair.

TILLY. Should I be making small-talk?

JOAN. No – no, don't bother with that.

TILLY. All right.

Will you both smile for a moment?

They both smile.

TILLY. You both have very nice teeth. Have you had dental work?

JOAN.	FRANCES.
No.	Yes.

TILLY. They don't have dental work in England, do they?

JOAN. No, they don't.

TILLY. I like bad teeth. So you look old when you're old, like you're supposed to.

JOAN. Yes.

TILLY. Maybe you could put on some music.

JOAN. What would you like to hear?

TILLY. Oh, anything.

Joan exits to put on a record: perhaps late 1960s, French.

Frances mounts Tilly.

Joan returns.

Frances unmounts Tilly.

TILLY. I love this album.

I'm suddenly tired. I think I'd better go now. Thank you for the New Zealand sandwiches. They were delicious. And it was so nice to meet you, Joan. Frances has told me a great deal about you. And it's all true.

JOAN. I'll show you to the door.

Good-bye.

TILLY. Good-bye.

FRANCES. Good-bye!

Tilly exits.

Joan looks after her as she goes.

Frances shuts the door.

FRANCES. So.

JOAN. So.

FRANCES. Now you know.

JOAN. Now I know.

FRANCES. And?

JOAN. It's strange, Frances. But I have this sexy sad feeling I've never had before. Like I'm in a European city before the war. We must invite her over again. Not for lunch. For dinner.

Let's open a window. It's hot in here.

FRANCES. Joan – I'm the one who was supposed to be having the affair. Me.

JOAN. I'm going to open a window.

She opens a window.

She has this remarkable smell – like old perfume – those little glass bottles with red thingmabobs that you squeeze like this –

Joan pretends to put perfume on her neck.

FRANCES. My mouth feels dry.

JOAN. In what way?

FRANCES. Like after you eat an almond. And before you want to kiss someone.

Joan moves in to kiss Frances.

Joan.

JOAN. What is it?

FRANCES. Let me smell your hair.

JOAN. Okay.

FRANCES. I can't smell it.

JOAN. What?

FRANCES. I can't smell it. Did you switch shampoos?

JOAN. No.

FRANCES. My God, Joan, I think I've lost my sense of smell.

JOAN. You're probably congested.

Here – smell my skin.

She does.

FRANCES. Nothing.

JOAN. Nothing? That's strange.

FRANCES. Nothing.

Tilly, alone

TILLY. Tonight I'm older than all the books.
I'm older than all the bricks in all the courtyards.
And I could write the saddest songs.

I want Frank.
I miss Frank.
I haven't seen Frank in two hours.

I wish I lived in a time when
people went to sea for years on end.
When there were still countries to be discovered.
I wish I could go on a ship for three years disguised as
a boy.
I wish I were there right now,
writing a long letter to Frank by candle-light.
I wish there was salt wind in my hair.

A church bell rings midnight.

It's my birthday.

Frank appears with flowers.

FRANK. Happy birthday.

TILLY. I was longing for you – and you appeared.

FRANK. Happy birthday, Tilly.

TILLY. Frank. I'm overwhelmed. You've made me very happy.

FRANK. I did?

TILLY. Yes!
You said happy birthday. It's my birthday. And I'm
happy. The way you're supposed to be on your birthday.
I feel like singing.

Julian plucks happy chords on his cello.

Everyone enters.

A Song

TILLY.
> I'm happy.
> I'm happy.
> Happy birthday.
> I'm happy.

FRANK.
> Happiness is bucktoothed.
> Happiness is bleeding.
> Happiness wears
> gold-capped teeth.

LORENZO.
> I was abandoned at a candy shop

JOAN.
> There's a word for it –

FRANCES.
> There's a word for it –

TILLY.	**JOAN.**
Remember?	Remember?
TILLY.	**JOAN.**
Remember?	Remember?

CHORUS.
> But not in English!
> Not in English!

TILLY.	**FRANCES.**
I smelled the ocean...	I smelled the ocean...

FRANK.
> What kind of a name is Frank....

JOAN.
> It's not really practical...

CHORUS.	**TILLY.**
All these windows	Happy birthday!
All these windows	Happy birthday!
All these windows	Happy birthday to me!

Tilly Becomes Happy

Frances, Joan, Tilly, and Lorenzo.

TILLY. I wanted to invite everyone I love to my birthday party.

Thank you all for coming.

Frank couldn't come. He has a stomach ache.

Would anyone care for an almond?

> *She passes almonds around in a little dish. Everyone eats one.*

What shall we play?

Frances – do you have an idea?

FRANCES. No.

JOAN. We could play duck duck goose.

TILLY. Oh, yes, oh, yes, let's play duck duck goose!!! Joan, you be it. Everyone sit in a circle.

LORENZO. I don't know your duck duck goose.

JOAN. Duck

Duck

Duck….

Goose!

> *(Joan tags Lorenzo.*
>
> *Lorenzo stands, not knowing what to do.*
>
> *She runs around the circle and sits in his spot.)*

TILLY. Lorenzo: you lost. That means you're "it."

Tap us on the head.

LORENZO. (*tapping Frances, then Joan*)

Person

person…

JOAN. It's duck duck goose.

You say duck duck goose.

LORENZO. I will play it my way.

Person… (*tapping Joan*)

Person... (*tapping Frances*)

(He tags Tilly.)

Goddess!

She chases him.

He tries to slow down so that he can turn around and kiss her.

TILLY. No, Lorenzo, run, run!

LORENZO. I love you!

JOAN. He goes in the mush-pot.

TILLY. That's right, Lorenzo. You'll have to go in the mush-pot.

LORENZO. I will not go in a mush-pot.

TILLY. Then run!

He doesn't move.

She chases him as he moves backwards, unwilling, to his spot.

TILLY. Now sit.

He sits in his spot.

Tilly is IT.

She looks around at the group.

TILLY. I can hardly play.
I'm so overcome by emotion
having all the people
I love in one room together.
Well, except for Frank.
I wish Frank were here too.
Let's make a little pretend spot for Frank.

Joan and Frances move to make a little pretend spot for Frank.

TILLY. Okay.
Duck

Duck

Duck

I just want to go on like this forever. I want it never to end.

She taps each on the head.

She is overwhelmed by their beauty.

This makes her happy.

Duck

Duck

Duck

Duck

I can't choose.

Duck

Duck

You're all so beautiful. I can't stand it.

Duck

Life really does have moments of transcendent beauty, doesn't it? At a party – each face – a flower – each face a –

Duck –

Duck

I'm so happy –

Duck

I'm so happy –

FRANCES. Are you all right, Tilly?

TILLY. I'm so happy – I don't know what to do…I'm sorry. I'm going to go in the other room to lie down. Joan, you be it.

Tilly exits. Joan gets up. They all look at each other.

Strange exultant music.

An intermission, or not. Preferably not.

PART 2

The Consequence of Tilly's Great Happiness

TILLY. Frank!

FRANK. What's wrong, Tilly? You look weird.

TILLY. I just had my birthday party. And Frank – I feel happy.

FRANK. Really?

TILLY. Yes. I feel – light. Giddy.

FRANK. You do?

TILLY. Yes. Frank – I think you've made me happy.

FRANK. But I wasn't at the party.

TILLY. Yes, I feel happy. I really do. How do you feel?

FRANK. I don't know.

TILLY. You look funny.

FRANK. I'm just – adjusting. To your being – happy.

TILLY. I feel – positively cheerful.

FRANK. Really – cheerful.

TILLY. My God, this is strange, I'm starting to feel happier, and happier, and happier – has my face changed –

She looks in the mirror.

She touches her face.

Do I look different – I feel – oh God, I feel – kiss me Frank –

FRANK. In a minute –

TILLY. Kiss me now – I want to share my great happiness with you –

FRANK. I don't feel – sexually aroused – at this juncture.

TILLY. Why, Frank?

FRANK. You look different.

TILLY. I'm happy!

FRANK. Yes.

TILLY. Don't you want me to be happy?

FRANK. I –

TILLY. Let's dance!

FRANK. I have a stomach ache.

TILLY. Frank?
Frank…

(She does a small dance of hopping towards him)

FRANK. You're saying my name wrong. That Frank was not me.
Tilly. I feel your happiness coming on like a great big storm.

TILLY. A storm?

FRANK. Your eyes aren't looking at me. They're looking at a great big storm of happiness. On the horizon. Can you see me?

He waves his hand in front of her face.

TILLY. I think I need to be alone with my happiness.
Or else with crowds of people in a public square.
Maybe I'll go to the bank and do some extra work.
Good-bye.

Tilly Confesses her Happiness to Lorenzo

TILLY. I wanted to tell you first. I'm happy.

LORENZO. What?

TILLY. Happy.

LORENZO. You have to admit this comes as something of a shock.

TILLY. I'm so sorry.

LORENZO. Happy?

TILLY. Happy.

LORENZO. No trace?

Every drop – gone?

TILLY. No trace.

I'm in love again.

Not with Frank.

With a woman who writes obituaries.

She has such a positive attitude.

I met her at the bank.

She was withdrawing all her money.

All of it.

Carpe diem, she said.

That's right, I said.

She said:

You really seem to enjoy your work.

I said: I do.

She said: I like that.

We wake up at 6am and go biking

before she finds out who's dead.

She writes the greatest obituaries.

They're not like the regular ones;

they've got flair. They're like little poems.

My God!

I am SO happy.

LORENZO. We can do a blood test...

TILLY. I don't need a blood test.

I'm happy.

LORENZO. Let's look out the window.

He holds her hand.

They look out the window. He directs her gaze.

Look at that old woman, walking home from the store by herself. For whom is she buying that gallon of milk? Where is her husband? It will be too much milk for her – she will think of her husband who is dead from the war. How much of the milk will sit, unused, in the afternoon, while she drinks her solitary cup of tea?

TILLY. The woman is sad. And beautiful. And she makes me happy.

LORENZO. Don't do this to me.

TILLY. I'm sorry. I told the bank I was happy and they won't pay for any more sessions. I'm cured.

Oh – here is the hair from my hair-cut. I saved it. For you. A relic from another time. Enjoy it.

She hands him a small packet of hair.

A tableau.

Joan and Frances and Tilly

Frances in her pajamas. Joan in her nurse's uniform.

Tilly appears on her bicycle.

TILLY. Hello! Thought I'd stop by! I'm on a very long bike ride!

JOAN & FRANCES. Hello.

TILLY. I wanted to tell you both. I'm happy.

FRANCES. Yes, you look – happy.

TILLY. I still love you both but in a happy way. I want to throw dinner parties and go hiking and plant nasturtiums. It's such a beautiful day out. Why are you both indoors on a day like this? Frances, you look terrible. What's wrong?

FRANCES. Nothing.

TILLY. Well, call me if you want to go biking! I can loan you my ten-speed!

Tilly exits.

Frances lies down on the ground.

FRANCES. My, God.

JOAN. Well, I'm happy that she's happy.

FRANCES. She's not happy. She's monstrous.

JOAN. Well. No use crying over spilt milk. You should go to work.

FRANCES. I should go to work.

You should go to work.

I'm taking a melancholy day.

JOAN. There's no such thing, is there?

FRANCES. There is when you own your own hair salon.

JOAN. I don't feel like going to work either.

JOAN & FRANCES. Let's stay home.

FRANCES. Let's lie down.

JOAN. Yes, let's.

> *They lie down in each other's arms.*

FRANCES. I can't smell anything.

JOAN. Still?

FRANCES. I had my morning coffee this morning
and I couldn't smell it.
It was like a commercial –
you know how in a commercial
you can see the people nodding and smiling
and smelling their coffee
but you can't smell what's on T.V.

JOAN. Do you have a sinus infection?

FRANCES. No.
Maybe the rest of my life will be like television.
No smell.

> *(Frances unravels. The following is not a reflective meditation.)*

FRANCES. Have you ever noticed that if you
listen to something,
then you *hear* it
and that *thing* you
hear is a *sound* ?

JOAN. Yes.

FRANCES. Okay. That's three different things! Listening,
hearing, and the thing you hear. Three things. But if
you try to *smell* something then you can *smell* it and
what you *smell* is a *smell*. They could only come up with
one word for it.

JOAN. Huh.

FRANCES. I mean – *why* do you think that is?

JOAN. I don't know.

FRANCES. Joan – my skin is dry.
Why is my skin so dry?
It's like bark.

JOAN. You're right. I'll put some lotion on it.

    I'm going to call in sick.

    She moves to call in sick. She stops.

JOAN. Wait.

    I can't call in sick.

    I'm a nurse.

    People need me.

    There's a man dying on the seventh floor.

FRANCES. I need you.

JOAN. I'm going to work now, Frances.

    I'll ask a doctor about your smell problem.

    Why don't you rake some leaves or shovel some snow or something like that?

FRANCES. I don't have a shovel.

    It's spring-time.

JOAN. Cheer up, Frances.

FRANCES. *Cheer up?*

JOAN. I'll call you from work.

    I love you, Frances.

FRANCES. Please, Joan. I have a bad feeling. I can't smell anything. How will I know if the house is burning down?

JOAN. You're not being rational.

FRANCES. I hate rational.

JOAN. You're a physicist.

FRANCES. Was! Was!

JOAN. Honestly, Frances, you're being a child!

FRANCES. Oh, go take care of sick people. I know how much you like to do that. Good-bye.

JOAN. Good-bye.

    Joan exits.

    Frances sits up.

    Frank appears in another window.

FRANCES. (*to the audience*)   **FRANK.** (*to the audience*)

I would like to curl up and
become a small thing.
About this big.

I would like to curl up and
become a small thing.
About this big.

(They pinch their fingers together – half an inch)

And still.
Very still.
Have you ever been
so melancholy,
that you wanted fit in the palm
of your beloved's hand?
And lie there, for
fortnights,
or decades, or the
length of time in between stars?
In complete silence?
Shhh. (*a finger to the lips*)

And still.
Very still.
Have you ever been
so melancholy,
that you wanted fit in the palm
of your beloved's hand?
And lie there, for
fortnights,
or decades, or the
length of time in between stars?
In complete silence?
Shhh.

Frances walks to a window and looks out.

Frank goes to see a therapist.

Frank goes to see Lorenzo the Unfeeling

LORENZO. Go on.

FRANK. I was hemming her pants, and I fell in love.

LORENZO. I know what love is!

FRANK. Excuse me?

LORENZO. Go on, go on.

Lorenzo is distracted.

He eats marzipan.

FRANK. She was so beautiful – when she was sad – I couldn't help myself – I wanted to bathe in her sadness like a bath –

LORENZO. Of course you did.

FRANK. She would cry sometimes, in her sleep. I put her tears in a little vial. I collected them.

LORENZO. Ah, like the Romans.

FRANK. What?

LORENZO. The Romans. Collected tears in little vials. Buried them with the dead.

FRANK. This vial is all I have left of her. Is that weird?

He produces a vial of tears.

LORENZO. Yes, it is weird. Would you like some candy? Marzipan. It's good.

FRANK. No, thank you. But you said the Romans did it.

LORENZO. Forget the Romans. Go on.

Lorenzo eats marzipan.

FRANK. I never loved someone so much. Now – she's gone – and I wish I were dead.

Lorenzo laughs.

FRANK. Why are you laughing?

LORENZO. Perhaps I am laughing because, I, too, have felt the way that you feel, Frank.

FRANK. Oh.

LORENZO. You seem – depressed.

FRANK. Maybe a little.

LORENZO. It is my medical opinion that you should go on medication. It's a very good medication. It will make you feel – very nice.

FRANK. I am sad because I fell out of love. I am not sad like: "I want to take medication."

LORENZO. Frank. Maybe you should have a little stay at the hospital.

FRANK. I don't want to stay at a hospital! I think I will move to another country. In French movies, people *die* of love. They *die* of it.

LORENZO. Frank. Frank. Poor Frank. Why don't you continue with your story.

FRANK. Well – one day – all at once – with no explanation – she was – happy. Cheerful, even. It was like a violent accident. A car wreck. We suddenly had nothing in common. I felt – so far away from her. Her face got red when she was happy, like a sweaty cow. And her voice got louder. And her eyes got glazed over, like a sweaty cow.

LORENZO. Yes! And how did that make you feel?

FRANK. Well, Tilly came home from her birthday party –

LORENZO. Tilly?

FRANK. That's the woman's name. Tilly.

LORENZO. I was at Tilly's birthday party! Not you!

FRANK. You know Tilly?

LORENZO. Do I know Tilly?
        DO I KNOW TILLY!

FRANK. This is outrageous. I am paying YOU!

LORENZO. Give me that vial of tears.

FRANK. No!

LORENZO. Give it here!

FRANK. No! It's mine! It's mine! I collected them!

LORENZO. Her tears belong to me!

Stirring fight music, from Julian.

They wrestle over the vial of tears.

This wrestling goes on for a good minute, with much swearing, name-calling and knocking over of furniture.

Joan appears at the door.

She knocks.

JOAN. *(from outside)* Is anything wrong?

She hears scuffling.

FRANK. Bastard!

LORENZO. Imbecile! Give it!

She enters.

JOAN. What's going on?

Lorenzo wrestles Frank to the ground and sits astride him.

LORENZO. Give me the vial or I will drool onto your face!

FRANK. I won't give it!

JOAN. *(over the shouting)* Lorenzo? Are you a doctor? Who is the doctor and who is the patient?

LORENZO. I am now going to let saliva drop down from my mouth – if you give me the vial, I will suck the drool back up – now – now!

FRANK. I won't! I won't!

JOAN. Should I call security?

LORENZO. Leave me alone with my patient, please. Give me the vial, Frank. Give it up.

FRANK. Her tears are mine!

LORENZO. I'm going to drool!

FRANK. *(to Joan)* I don't know who you are – but please – help me – take this vial – And run! Run! It belongs to a woman named Tilly –

Frank reaches towards Joan.

Lorenzo pulls on Frank's legs.

Joan takes the vial.

She looks at the audience.

A tableau.

Strange music, from Julian, on his cello.

The Vial of Tears

Joan, holding the vial of tears, walks towards Frances.

FRANCES. What's that?

JOAN. Tilly's tears.

FRANCES. Give it.

JOAN. Why?

Joan gives Frances the vial.

Frances drinks the tears.

JOAN. Frances! Honestly!!!

They look at each other.

Joan holds out her hand for the vial.

Music from Julian.

A song from the company

The music from Julian continues.

Joan, Frances, and Lorenzo appear.

FRANK, JOAN, FRANCES, AND LORENZO.
Oh, for the melancholy Tilly!
Why did she become so silly?
We loved her when she had
the capacity for pity!
Oh for the melancholy Tilly!

JOAN & FRANCES.	**LORENZO & FRANK.**
Stars a cause	Junk-food a cause.
Love a cause	Cheetos and Doritos
Death a cause	and cheddar Goldfish a cause.

Oh for the melancholy Tilly! Oh for the melancholy Tilly!

FRANK, JOAN, FRANCES, & LORENZO.
Life used to be so slow
Life used to be so sweet
Life used to be bannisters
And rain drenched cobbled streets!
Oh, for the melancholy Tilly!

JOAN & FRANCES.	**LORENZO & FRANK.**
Stars a cause	Narrow streets
Love a cause	and telegrams
Death a cause	and cheddar Goldfish a cause.

Oh, for the melancholy
    Tilly!

> *Tilly walks across the stage holding a helium balloon.*

> *They look at her.*

FRANK, JOAN, FRANCES, & LORENZO.
Life used to be so slow

Life used to be so sweet
Life used to be balconies
And paintings by Magritte!
Oh, for the melancholy Tilly!
Oh, for the melancholy Tilly!

The song ends.

A tableau. A suspended moment.

Frances looks at everyone.

The light changes. Frances has a revelation.

Lights glow on Frances. She has a desire to disappear.

FRANCES. Oh!

Frances rides on a window out through a door,

or walks through a balcony

or she makes a very long cross.

Whatever it is —

she does something melancholy, slow and theatrical.

Full of longing, mysterious, simple, riveting.

She slows down time for us.

She makes us wonder.

This only lasts about six seconds.

We watch her.

Joan reveals a terrible secret to Tilly

At a café. Joan and Tilly.

Tilly drinks a coke with a straw.

Joan wears dark glasses and a scarf.

TILLY. And I continue to get happier and happier and happier. It's like a sickness. No one likes to hear about it. A brick could fall on my head and it would somehow increase my pleasure. Joan – is something wrong?

JOAN. Well, yes.

TILLY. Oh, I'm sorry. I've been so self-absorbed. What is it?

JOAN. It's Frances.

TILLY. Is something wrong with Frances? Is she ill?

JOAN. Not exactly.

TILLY. What is it?

JOAN. It's – she's – she's turned into an almond.

    Pause.

TILLY. What?

JOAN. It's the oddest thing. I came home from work. When I left she was lying on the couch, looking out the window. When I came back, there was an almond on the pillow.

TILLY. No!

JOAN. Yes.

TILLY. I'm so sorry.

JOAN. I feel terrible. She told me not to go to work that day. She'd lost her sense of smell. But I went to work. I left her.

TILLY. It's not your fault, Joan. You can't blame yourself for this.

JOAN. She lies in bed, so still, so quiet – so oval-shaped. She looks like she's about to cough, but she can't, because she's an almond.

TILLY. Can I see her?

JOAN. Of course.

By the bedside of Frances the almond

Joan enters, carrying a small white pillow, upon which is laid an almond.

Joan puts down the pillow.

Tilly kneels beside the almond.

TILLY. Oh, Frances. Is it my fault? Have I brought you to this? Don't speak, Frances.

JOAN. Any sign?

TILLY. No.

Tilly pets the almond.

TILLY. I can't help but feel that this is somehow my fault.
Do you have any salt, Joan?

JOAN. I'll get some.

TILLY. I'll salt you, Frances. That will make you feel better. Salted almonds are so much better than plain ones.

Joan enters with salt.

Tilly puts some salt on Frances the almond.

TILLY. How does that feel?
You're beautiful, Frances.

(to Joan, in a whisper)

Are you sure this is Frances?

JOAN. It seems like Frances, doesn't it?

TILLY. Yes.

I'm so sorry Joan.
Talk to me Frances.
It's Tilly.
Are you all right in there?
So quiet.
So quiet.
What are you thinking about Frances?
Frances?

I love you.

Frances!

How do you talk to an almond?

She tosses the almond up in the air three times.

Whee!

Whee!

Wasn't that fun Frances?

You're so little now.

And so light.

The good news is that I'm happy, Frances.

Everyone around me seems so sad

and I just can't relate.

I feel like a little red sports car.

Can you hear me Frances?

Give me a sign.

Come on, Frances.

She listens to the almond.

Joan – what reason do you have to believe that Frances actually turned *into* an almond? I mean – is it possible – that she ran away – and put an almond on the chair – as a kind of – going away present? Like a mint – at a hotel?

JOAN. She wouldn't leave me.

TILLY. I'm going to taste her.

Joan is shocked.

Tilly licks Frances the almond.

TILLY. It tastes – sort of like Frances. I don't know – if Frances were an almond is this how she would taste? About like this?

Tilly licks the almond again, puzzled.

TILLY. Is it – familiar? I don't know.

JOAN. I haven't called the police yet.

TILLY. Much better to leave them out of this, I think.

They regard the almond.

They blow on the almond.

They knock on the almond.

JOAN. Maybe we should eat her.

TILLY. No!

JOAN. She would want it that way. To become a part of us. She can't think! She can't feel! She's not even – a vegetable! She's – she's a nut, Tilly.

TILLY. Joan – do you think there are others – like Frances?

A letter is shoved under a door.

JOAN. What is it?

TILLY. A letter.

JOAN. Read it.

The music of intrigue, from Julian, on his cello.

TILLY. If you are experiencing any form of melancholy: stay in your home. I repeat: STAY IN YOUR HOME. Occupy your mind. Occupy your hands. Do not look out the window in the afternoon dreaming of the past or far off things or absent people or dead people or the sea. People experiencing melancholy have been turning into almonds on the street.

Do not eat these almonds. Do not step on these almonds. If you DO find an almond, or if a family member BECOMES an almond, DO put him or her in a zip-lock bag and deposit it in the nearest mailbox.

JOAN. Who's it from?

TILLY. Anonymous.

Tilly and Joan slowly turn and look at each other, frightened.

They look at the almond.

A thin beam of light on the almond.

Inside the almond

Frances appears in a well of light, behind a window.

FRANCES. *(to the audience)* It's nice in here.
It's quiet.

Lorenzo

Lorenzo, walking down the street,
stepping on almonds.

LORENZO. (*to the audience*)
  It is – an epidemic!
  The streets are littered –
  littered – with almonds!
  I stepped on one –
  I stepped on two –
  on my way here.
  I crushed them
  under my shoe.
  See?

Joan at work, the night-shift

Joan takes Frances out of her pocket.

Hi, Frances.

I miss you, Frances.

Everything is going to be all right, Frances. I promise you.

I'm a nurse. I can fix things.

Now….

Let's see.

Cures for Melancholy:

Food a remedy.

Music a remedy.

Love – a remedy.

Okay.

Causes of Melancholy:

Food a cause.

Music a cause.

Love – a cause.

Well. That's a problem.

Tilly goes to Frank's Tailor Shop

TILLY. Frank. I had to see you.

FRANK. I'm busy. I'm sewing.

TILLY. I know you don't want to see me.

But I'm in trouble, Frank.

My friend – has turned into an almond. And I'm afraid that it's my fault.

FRANK. What?

TILLY. And meanwhile, I feel lighter and lighter.

I am trying to cultivate – a sensation of – gravity.

But nothing helps.

FRANK. An almond?

TILLY. Yes.

Frank – you can fix most things.

If a jacket doesn't fit – you can fix it.

If a dress has a hole – you can mend it.

How can I fix Frances?

FRANK. Frances?

TILLY. Yes, Frances.

Frank, you've turned pale.

FRANK. Tilly – there is something I have never told you because the memory was too painful. I was separated at birth from my twin sister – Frances.

Stirring music from Julian.

We were abandoned at a toy store in an unspecified Scandinavian country. My mother – melancholy by nature – sailed the fjords and never came back. My father – a toy-maker – longed to follow her. And so he hid us in large gift-wrapped packages and stowed us away on ships, bound for America.

Do you know the pain of being gift-wrapped at a young age? My first memory is of being opened.

My sister – Frances was her name – was shipped to New Jersey. And I was sent to Illinois. But all my life, I have been haunted – longing for my lost Scandinavian sister, Frances.

TILLY. My God!
  You look exactly like her!*

FRANK. So it's true.

TILLY. Why didn't you tell me sooner?
  Now it's too late.

FRANK. My sister – has turned into – an almond?

TILLY. I'm afraid so.

FRANK. How did this happen?

FRANCES. *(from a well of light behind a window)*
  Because the quiet was all she owned
  she walked to an almond tree
  undid the branches.....
  and lying down
  became an almond.

TILLY. We have to get her back.
  How do you get to where almonds are?
  Can you climb a tree?
  Can you sail there?

FRANK. Let me think.

TILLY. There's a word – in another language – it means –
  to be so melancholy that you turn into an inanimate
  object.

FRANK. What is the word?

TILLY. I don't know.

FRANK. What is the language?

TILLY. A dead language, I think.

FRANK. Don't worry. We'll find her.

TILLY. Oh, Frank.
  I've missed you.

  They embrace.

---

* *Depending on casting, you might change this line to:* "My God!
You look nothing like her!" *Or even:* "My God, you look a
little bit like her!"

Tilly weeps tears into Frank's suit.

FRANK. Tilly? Are you crying?

TILLY. Yes.

FRANK. We have to collect your tears.

TILLY. What?

Joan, Lorenzo, Frank, Tilly and the Almond

TILLY. We're all here with a common purpose.

    To get Frances back.

LORENZO. *(to Frank)*

    You again.

FRANK. Let's be friends, Lorenzo, for the sake of Frances.

        (turning towards the almond)

    This is my sister?

JOAN. I'm afraid so.

FRANK. Can I hold her?

JOAN. Of course.

        Joan hands Frank the almond.

FRANK. Frances!

TILLY. Do you recognize her?

FRANK. I think so.

JOAN. Frances.

    I'd rather be an almond with you

    than be a person with me.

    Tell me how to be an almond.

    Tell me, tell me, tell me.

    I'll be quiet.

TILLY. Can you hear anything?

JOAN. No.

    I'm sorry I told you to cheer up, Frances.

    That was stupid.

        A moment of respect for Joan's loss.

FRANK. Tilly, I believe you have the vial of tears.

TILLY. Frank has an idea.

FRANK. If we each drink one sip from the vial of tears, we
    will become almonds, and we will find Frances.

LORENZO. I don't want to be an almond. I like my body!

Tilly stands on a chair.

She delivers a rousing speech.

TILLY. Lorenzo. When someone in your social circle becomes so melancholy that they stop moving, it is your duty as a human being to *go find them.* It is not enough to seek medical attention. It is not enough to ask them how they are feeling. You must go where they are and *get* them. It is up to *all of us* to save Frances. It is part of the social contract.

JOAN, LORENZO & FRANK. It is?

TILLY. It should be!

LORENZO. I go where Tilly goes.

FRANK. Okay, then.

We'll put Frances in the center of the circle.

They put Frances in the center of the circle.

They each drink from the vial of tears.

They all hold hands. They shut their eyes.

The lights fade to blackness for the first and only time in the play.

An extended note on the cello.

A CHANT IN THE DARK

(Somewhere between a madrigal and a liturgical chant.)

TILLY, FRANK, JOAN & LORENZO. Cellos and the color blue.
Olives.
Vespers. Rain in the middle of a tree branch.
Windows. The sound of crickets,
memories of an unseen lighthouse.
A broken fence, a broken onion,
lost objects, windows, dust,
hallways with a particular smell
which you will never re-visit,

most forms of longing,
windows, wind, windows.

> *The lights go up.*

> *Frances has appeared in the center of the circle.*

> *Everyone gasps.*

FRANCES. Am I in the mush pot?
   Is this duck duck goose?
JOAN. Frances!
FRANCES. Joan!
TILLY. Frances!
FRANCES. Tilly!
FRANK. Frances! It's Frank, your long lost brother.
FRANCES. Frank, my long lost brother!

> *Frank and Frances embrace.*

Where did you – ? How did you – ?

FRANK.	**FRANCES.**
All my life –	All my life –
Something missing.	Something missing.

(to each other)

When you were a child
   did you
look out the window at
   the moon –

Yes – and wonder
if you were looking
out the window at the
   moon

at the very same time –   at the very same time –
only in New Jersey?   only in Illinois?
Yes.   Yes.

FRANCES. My God!
   Frank!
FRANK. Frances!

LORENZO. Wait –

a moment –

a moment –

are we – all of us – now almonds?

FRANK. How could we know?

JOAN. How could we know?

FRANK. Is this how an almond looks to another almond?

They look at one another.

They rush to a mirror.

They look in the mirror for a good long while.

TILLY. Did Frances come to us or did we come to Frances? Frances?

FRANCES. I don't know.

JOAN. Perhaps it's best not to know.

(Pause.)

FRANCES. *(to JOAN)*

Did you love me Joan when I went into a deep well of silence?

JOAN. Yes.

A silence. Then, stirring music from Julian.

They all hear the music, for the first time.

This makes them happy.

TILLY. Someone's playing music!

They all notice Julian, for the first time.

TILLY. *(to the musician)* That's beautiful.

JULIAN. Thank you.

Julian continues to play.

TILLY. What's your name?

JULIAN. Julian.**

** *Or the cellist's real name*

FRANK. Hello.

JOAN. Hello!

FRANCES. Hello!

LORENZO. Hello!

Julian stops playing.

JULIAN. Hello.

LORENZO. Excuse me, but would you mind telling us – are we almonds? Do we look like almonds? Are we in Illinois?

JULIAN. I don't know.

TILLY. Julian – can you play something happy?

JULIAN. I think so.

It's difficult on a cello.

Julian begins to play a waltz.

Frances catches hold of Joan.

FRANCES. Joan. I can smell your hair.

JOAN. Oh, Frances!

LORENZO. Can almonds smell? Am I an almond?

TILLY. Lorenzo! For the last time. We don't care if we're almonds. The important thing is that we're together.

A waltz comes up on a Victrola.

Frank – I adore you.

Tilly catches hold of Frank.

FRANK. Oh, Tilly.

FRANCES. Oh, Frank.

JOAN. Oh, Frances.

FRANCES. Oh, Joan.

LORENZO. Oh, Julian.

Lorenzo catches hold of Julian.

They are happy.

They all dance a waltz.

The chandeliers glimmer.

The lights fade out.

The end.